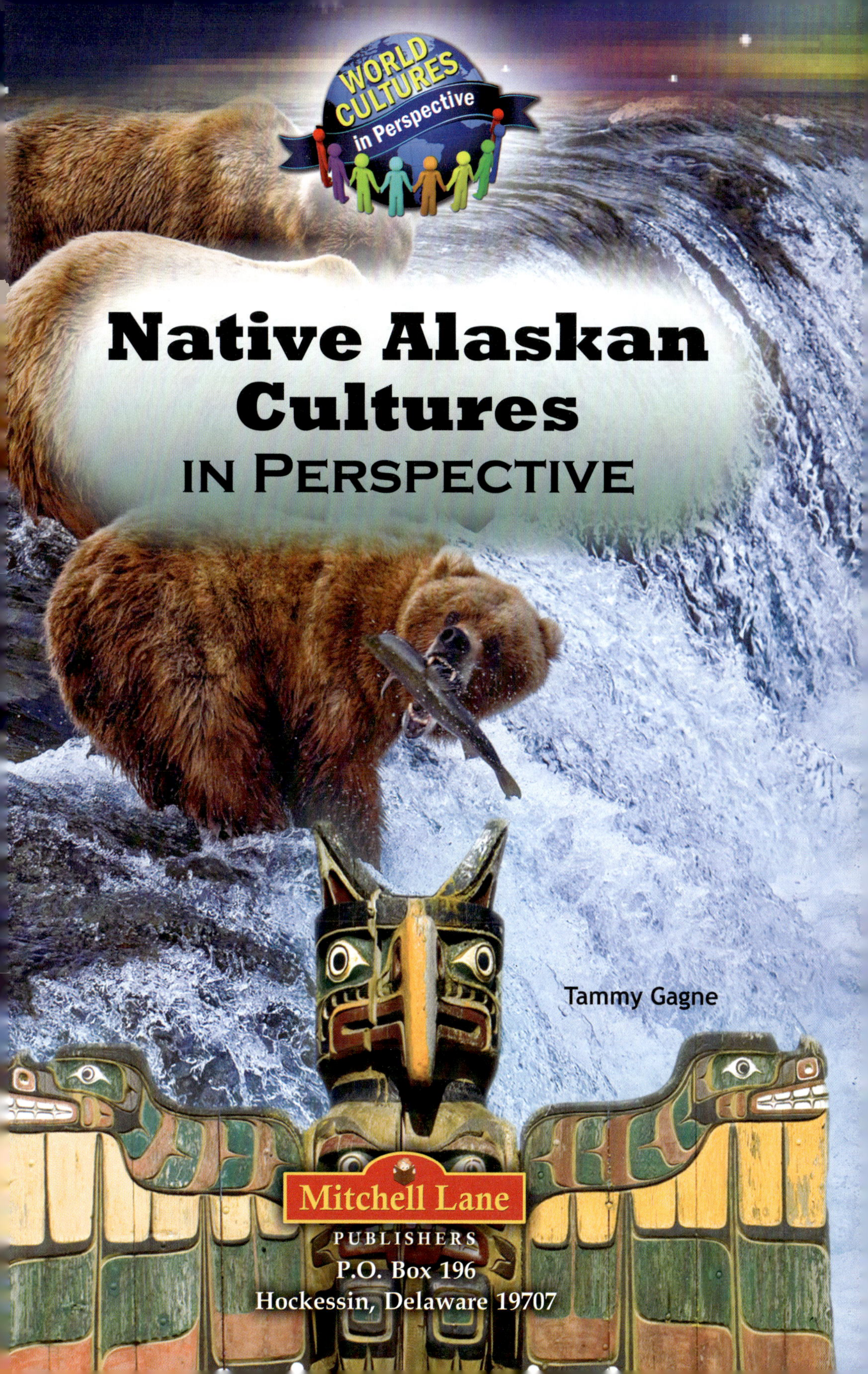

Native Alaskan Cultures
IN PERSPECTIVE

Tammy Gagne

Mitchell Lane
PUBLISHERS
P.O. Box 196
Hockessin, Delaware 19707

WORLD CULTURES in Perspective

Brazilian Cultures in Perspective

Caribbean Cultures in Perspective

East Asian Cultures in Perspective

Islamic Culture in Perspective

Israeli Culture in Perspective

Louisiana Creole & Cajun Cultures in Perspective

Native Alaskan Cultures in Perspective

North African Cultures in Perspective

Polynesian Cultures in Perspective

Southeast Asian Cultures in Perspective

Mitchell Lane
PUBLISHERS

 Printed and bound in the United States of America.

Printing 1 2 3 4 5 6 7 8 9

Library of Congress Cataloging-in-Publication Data
Gagne, Tammy.
Native Alaskan cultures in perspective / by Tammy Gagne.
pages cm. — (World cultures in perspective)
Includes bibliographical references and index.
ISBN 978-1-61228-561-0 (library bound)
1. Alaska Natives—Juvenile literature. 2. Alaska Natives—Social life and customs—Juvenile literature. 3. Alaska Natives—Social conditions—Juvenile literature. 4. Alaska—Social life and customs—Juvenile literature. 5. Alaska—Social conditions—Juvenile literature. 6. Alaska—Ethnic relations—Juvenile literature. I. Title.
E78.A3G34 2015
305.8009798—dc23
2014019901

eBook ISBN: 9781612286006

PUBLISHER'S NOTE: This story is based on the author's extensive research, which she believes to be accurate. Documentation of this research is on page 61.

The Internet sites referenced herein were active as of the publication date. Due to the fleeting nature of some web sites, we cannot guarantee they will all be active when you are reading this book.

PBP

CONTENTS

INTRODUCTION

When we think of Native American cultures, a variety of tribes instantly come to mind. The Navajo, Cherokee, and Sioux are just a few Native peoples that have been part of the United States since even before the United States itself existed. Some parts of Native American cultures have become so ingrained in the daily lives of Americans that they may not even realize their origin. For example, the words *chipmunk*, *hickory*, and *persimmon* all came from Native American languages. But many Americans forget that Native American tribes stretch as far north as the northernmost US state—Alaska.

This remote part of the United States is home to numerous Native American cultures, each one at least a little different from the rest. Because of the challenges the Alaskan climate and terrain present, some of these tribes have limited contact with the others—and with the tribes in the lower states. Harsh winters and long distances led many Native Alaskan tribes to become fiercely resourceful and independent. But each tribe is still a part of American history and Native American culture as a whole.

CHAPTER ONE
The Athabascans

Traditional Athabascans lived in small groups that fished, hunted, and trapped together. This group relied heavily on sharing. The hunters' job was to find the food and to share it with nearby hunters and their tribes. Sharing was a basic way of life. The practice has been passed down to modern Athabascans. *Anchorage Daily News* columnist Julia O'Malley has written about her Aunt Barbara who still follows the old custom. "One filet of the first salmon of the season must be given away as a matter of custom," she explains.[1]

Ricky Gease, executive director of the Kenai River Sportfishing Association, urges people to be respectful of the Native tradition. "It's a two-way, not a one-way street," he insists.[2] He points out that a person who receives fish doesn't have to give fish in return. But another gift—like homemade jam or jelly, for instance—is considered a polite gesture.

Aunt Barbara sees sharing as a positive thing. "Fish is best fresh and shared," she states. "There is nothing like fish to bring people together."[3]

The Athabascan people once occupied a large region of Alaska. Members of this group, who call themselves Dena (meaning "the people"), could be found in the Brooks Mountains, the northernmost section of the Rocky Mountains. They extended all the way down to the Kenai Peninsula, just south of Anchorage. Groups of twenty to forty Athabascans made their homes along the rivers running through this region. They moved with the seasons in search of food.

Like many Native Alaskans, Athabascans used a variety of natural resources to make the tools they needed for daily life. They used wood and stone, as well as animal antlers and bones to make these tools, with which they then built houses and boats, and made

An Athabascan fish trap looks a bit different from traps found elsewhere in the United States. The people designed this and other important tools based on the available natural resources.

clothing, cooking utensils, and snowshoes. They used birch trees, cottonwood trees, and moose hides for making canoes.

The Athabascans made warm moccasins and boots from the hides of caribou and moose. Both men and women knew how to sew these items, but women did most of this work.

One of the most interesting things about Athabascan culture is that women determine the structure of the clans. Children belong to the mothers' clans instead of the fathers'. There are only two exceptions, the Holikachuk and the Deg Hit'an. Traditionally, the center of most Athabascan clans was a woman, her brother, and

Staying warm during the winter months was a big priority for early Native American tribes. They relied heavily on the pelts of animals such as wolves and foxes for this purpose.

their two families. In many cases the woman's husband and her brother would become hunting partners. This arrangement would begin with the woman's marriage and last for the rest of their lives. In many clans the brother also plays a key role in raising his sister's children. Since he knows more about the clan's history and customs than their own father, it is their uncle's job to teach them about life as an Athabascan.

Little by little, the ways of the Athabascan people have been replaced with modern methods. Although change can sometimes be seen as progress, in some cases it can wipe out much of a group's culture. The Athabascans' languages are in danger of being lost without the help of those who can still speak them. The problem is that so few people still do.

The Siletz Dee-ni language, also known as Coastal Athabascan, was once so common that it was spoken from Alaska all the way south to the west coast of the United States. Today, only five people are known to speak Siletz Dee-ni fluently. One of them is Bud Lane, who is creating an online dictionary with the help of the Living Tongues Institute. The resource includes more than 10,000 audio recordings, which have taken Lane seven years to log. And it still isn't finished.

Lane has heard from many people who want to help him with his project. "We don't know where it's going to go," he admits. But for now, the goal is to hold on to what still exists, "creating a pool of speakers large enough that it won't go away," he explains.[4]

The language isn't always an easy one for new learners. Sonya Moody-Jurado attends classes taught by Lane. She said, "There are a couple of sounds that are nowhere in the English language, like you're going to spit, almost. Learning along with her grandson, she notes, "kids seem much more open to that."[5]

David Harrison is an associate professor of linguistics at Swarthmore College in Pennsylvania. He has helped the Siletz tribe with the dictionary. Harrison hopes that other Native American tribes take similar steps to preserve their languages with a project like the Siletz dictionary. "It's become a model of how you do it," he states.[6]

The Last Great Race on Earth

Athabascans traveled through snow on sleds. You have probably seen dog sled races in movies and on television. Known as mushing, this sport can be traced back to the Thule culture (the ancestors of the Inuit) in the middle of the 12th century. Like the Thule, the Athabascans were known for keeping packs of dogs to pull their sleds. Today mushing is the state sport of Alaska.

The Iditarod Trail Sled Dog Race has been held each year in Alaska since 1973. The word Iditarod means "a far and distant place" in the Athabascan language. This definition is fitting, as the brutal race takes the competing mushers and their dogs from Anchorage all the way to Nome—more than 1,000 miles (about 1,600 kilometers). Of the thirty-five men who took part in the very first event, only twenty-two of them finished. And it took the winner twenty days to reach the end of the trail. Modern mushers have completed the course in less than half that time. Dallas Seavey holds the record of finishing the fastest. In 2014, he managed the feat in just eight days, thirteen hours.[7]

Originally, the trail was used to deliver mail and other supplies to the Alaskan people. But in 1925, a group of sick children in Nome became very ill. That year, the mushers who traveled the route were racing to their destination to save lives. The Iditarod was created as a way to honor their success in getting the medication to the sick children who needed it. Today, many people call the Iditarod "The Last Great Race on Earth."

The 2014 winner of the Iditarod Trail Sled Dog Race was Dallas Seavey. He is seen here in Nome with two of his canine companions—Beatle and Reef—who helped him make it to the finish line.

Chapter Two
The Unangax and Alutiiq

The Unangax and Alutiiq people came from southern and southwestern areas of Alaska. Out of necessity, they occupied the coastal regions and Alaskan islands.

Because Alaska is so close to Russia, the Unangax and Alutiiq cultures adopted many customs from that country. Although Alaska is now part of the United States, the territory belonged to Russia until 1867. The mixing of the cultures, though, continues to this day. Members of these Native Alaskan clans cook many Russian dishes, for example. The Unangax and Alutiiq also use many Russian words in their languages. Each village in this region even has an Orthodox Church for Natives who follow the Russian Orthodox religion.

Many Russians and Natives have intermarried. Dr. Lydia Black, a local historian, explains, "Very few Russian women came to Alaska."[1] As a result, many of the Russian men married Native Alaskans.

Tania Chichkenoff was born in Alaska. Although she has both Russian and Native Alaskan ancestors, she grew up in the Orthodox faith. "We were born not knowing that there was any other," she recalls. "We live in a remote, remote village, and the only thing was Orthodox . . . and we've kept it. I have eight children and thirty-six grandchildren, and they've all been baptized Orthodox."[2]

Yury Lisyankshy was a Russian Navy officer and explorer who traveled to Alaska.

The territory of this group extends from the inlet known as Prince William Sound off the southern coast of the state to the tip of the Aleutian Islands. Although many people refer to the Native islanders as the Aleut, tribe members do not use this name. They call themselves the Unangax. A small number of Unangax also live on nearby Bering Island, which is still part of Russia.

Today life is pretty peaceful on Alaska's islands, but in the 1940s, this region was anything but serene. During World War II, the United States evacuated Native Alaskans living on the islands, sending them to camps on the mainland. A total of 881 Unangax from nine different villages were among the uprooted people. Each one was allowed to take just a single suitcase. The United States National Park Service website describes the scene as the Natives were ushered away onto crowded transport ships. "Heartbroken, [the] villagers watched as US servicemen set their homes and church afire so they would not fall into Japanese hands."[3]

The conditions at the camps were even worse than on the ships. The relocated Natives lacked warm clothing, proper food, and

Alaskans from the Aleutian city of St. Paul were forced from their homes during World War II. Some of them are seen here on the US Delarof as they head to internment camps in southeast Alaska.

clean water. They had no plumbing or electricity. The islanders remained in the camps for two years with little to no medical care. Over time diseases like pneumonia and tuberculosis began to spread, claiming the lives of the youngest and the oldest people. In all, seventy-four people died. Since many of them were elders, much of the history and culture of the Unanagax people died with them.

One of the people who lived to tell about the experience was Bill Tcheripanoff, Sr., of Akutan Island. "In 1942, my wife and our four children were whipped away from our home . . . all our possessions were left. . . . I tried to pretend it was really a dream and this could not happen to me and my dear family."[4]

The Alutiiq people are known by many different names. Anthrolpologists divide them into three sub-groups: the Chugachmiut, the Unegkurmiut, and the Koniagmiut. The Native

Alaskan clans have different names for themselves. Each one is based on where the clan was from, adding the suffix "-miut" (meaning "the people of"). For instance, the Koniagmiut are also known as the Qikertarmiut, which means "people of the large island."

The various clans among both the Unangax and Alutiiq were especially respectful of one another. For example, they divided the land into territories. This arrangement kept one tribe from intruding upon another's natural resources such as fish and plants.

The Alutiiq stand out for their unique housing, which interestingly didn't stand out at all. Their homes, known as ciqlluaq, were built partially underground. This design helped to shield them from the harsh elements of the area. Natives entered the dwellings by way of ladders from their tops. Because the roof of each ciqlluaq was covered with grass, people who didn't know they were there might not even see them.

Alaska became a focal point for military activity during World War II. During the Aleutian Islands campaign, the US recaptured the islands of Attu and Kiska from the Japanese. The soldiers seen here with their 50mm machines gun are searching the sky for enemy aircraft.

Although the world knows how the Alutiiq fished and how they built their homes, many other parts of their culture aren't as well known. Sven Haakanson wants to recover the missing pieces. He is the executive director of the Alutiiq Museum. Haakanson shares, "We've been working with elders, museum collections, we've been documenting our language, we've been documenting pretty much everything that has been lost."[5] He knows that if he and others who care about the culture don't act fast enough, some things may be lost forever.

Like the Athabascan people, the Alutiiq language faces a particular risk of becoming extinct. In 1999, only twenty-four people could speak the language fluently. It only took ten years for that number to be cut in half. Haakanson reports, "It's been a real challenge for us to try to maintain our language, but also trying to preserve it."[6]

Haakanson himself is learning about his own history in the process. "I grew up not knowing much about my culture, not knowing who we were in terms of our 7,500 years of history, and what it really meant. . . ." He adds that through the museum's efforts, "[W]e will hopefully continue for the next century building and putting that knowledge back into a context where it becomes commonplace knowledge, instead of museum knowledge. . . ."[7]

Native American art has been known to fetch some high prices. Carved wooden masks, similar to this one owned by artist Perry Eaton, have sold for around $30,000.

Unangax Culture Camp

People interested in learning more about Unangax culture can sign up for an educational experience called the Urban Unangax Culture Camp. Each summer about 200 adults and children visit the tribe's central headquarters in Anchorage, Alaska, for the event.

A wide range of ages are welcome at the camp. Kids ten and under attend shorter, morning sessions where they learn about the tribe's history through stories told by the elders and about the Unangax language and food. Older kids stay all day. They can choose from a wider variety of hands-on activities including dance, drum-making, and gut-sewing. Those interested in a bigger project can even learn how to build a kayak. Adult-only classes are held in the evenings. Grownups can attend then or during the day with the kids. But during the day, the children are the main focus.

Camp ends with a closing ceremony to share what everyone has learned. Community members and some of the campers prepare traditional dishes for the celebration. Art projects are displayed. Songs and dances are performed. Even the kayak is shown off as participants head to a nearby lake for anyone who wants a ride in it.

Chapter Three
The Yup'ik and Cup'ik

While some Native clans are named after their locations, others are named for their languages. This is the case with the Native Alaskans from the southwest part of the state: the Yup'ik and Cup'ik people. You may also hear this group of Native Alaskans referred to as Eskimos. Like other Native Alaskans, the traditional lives of the Yup'ik and Cup'ik relied heavily on hunting and fishing for survival. Both skills were passed from older generations to the younger clan members.

Like the Athabascans, these clans moved according to where they could find food. But the living arrangements of the Yup'ik and Cup'ik differed greatly from other Native tribes. In many communities, the men lived separately from the women. Once a boy was old enough to leave his mother, he would move to a qasgiq, the name given to the men's residence. Although women did not live in the qasgiq, they were still responsible for cooking for the men. The qasgiq was where the tribes gathered for their ceremonies and other celebrations. Women and children of the

Although the men and women lived separately, they had many interactions. The women cooked for the male tribe members on a daily basis. And everyone gathered frequently for celebrations at the qasgiq—the men's lodge.

Yup'ik and Cup'ik lived in smaller homes called enas. They looked similar to qasgiqs but were only about half the size.

Like the homes of the Alutiiq, both the qasgiq and the ena were built with roof entrances. This design made it easier for tribe members to enter and exit during the winter months when large amounts of snow fell.

Yup'ik and Cup'ik hunted with spears, harpoons, and bows. They also used bows as instruments of warfare. At home, female Yup'ik and Cup'ik tribe members used a fan-shaped knife called an uluaq. Women also used stones, bones, and walrus ivory to make sewing tools.

Men led the tribes. Women were left in charge of raising the children, preparing food, and sewing while the men hunted.

The Yup'ik and Cup'ik had many cultural traditions, including dancing. But in 1914, Quaker missionaries who had settled in the area banned the dancing. They saw the custom as evil.

Over time the Quakers' views became ingrained in the Native people as well. Natives didn't just stop dancing; they changed the way they saw the activity. They went from expressing their thankfulness for good fortune through dancing to thinking of dancing as devil worship.

Theresa Arevgaq John is a Yup'ik Eskimo. She is also a Native studies professor at the University of Alaska in Fairbanks. She explains that a large part of the Eskimo identity was destroyed with the banning of dance. "It was our only way of prayer. Can you imagine someone coming in and saying your way is wrong?"[1]

Today tribe members are free to take part in traditional dance, and many Natives do. Mike Ulroan never knew a time when dancing wasn't allowed. By the time he was born in the 1980s, dancing was once again a regular part of life in his Cup'ik Eskimo village of Chevak. To this day he continues to dance with several groups. "It's just a way to make me feel happy," he said. "With the movements we do, we push away bad spirits and keep away sickness."[2]

The effects left by the missionaries are undeniable. Dance instructor Richard Atoruk insists, "I think we lost a lot of our history because the missionaries came." But, he adds, "Now it's coming back."[3]

The unique design of the uluaq helped early Alaskan women prepare food from the region. The curved blade helped them cut through the skin and bones of fish.

An Unexpected Find

In 2008, unusual objects began washing ashore in Quinhagak, a village on the Bering Sea. The items were soon linked to the Yup'ik people. One of the most surprising things about the objects was their age. Anthropologist Rick Knecht, who dated the artifacts, determined they were created before the Europeans first had contact with the Yup'ik people in the 1800s.

Knecht remembers, "I had a project on Nunivak (Island) at the time, so I stopped by to have a look. . . . This is easily the largest collection of pre-contact Yup'ik material anywhere."[4] The size of the discovery also made it an important one. It consisted of thousands of items dating from between 1350 and 1670.

One of the most perplexing parts of the find was the material from which many of the items were made. These curious objects were constructed of wood, a substance that usually decays in a matter of decades. "Because it's been in permafrost up until now, the level of preservation is just marvelous," observes Knecht. "Eighty percent of what we're finding is wood or other organics. A lot of them are preserved to the extent that they still have original paint on them. For all practical purposes, we're looking at new wood."[5]

Other items that surprisingly survived the centuries included woven grass, clothing, dolls, and even human hair. "We have scraps of sealskin clothing with original needle holes," Knecht notes. "The grass basketry—sometimes the grass is still a little green. You can see it fade as oxygen hits it when it's uncovered. There's cordage, ropes made from grass and roots. It's very rare to find them. . . . We found some amazing pieces. . . . I've never seen anything like it."[6]

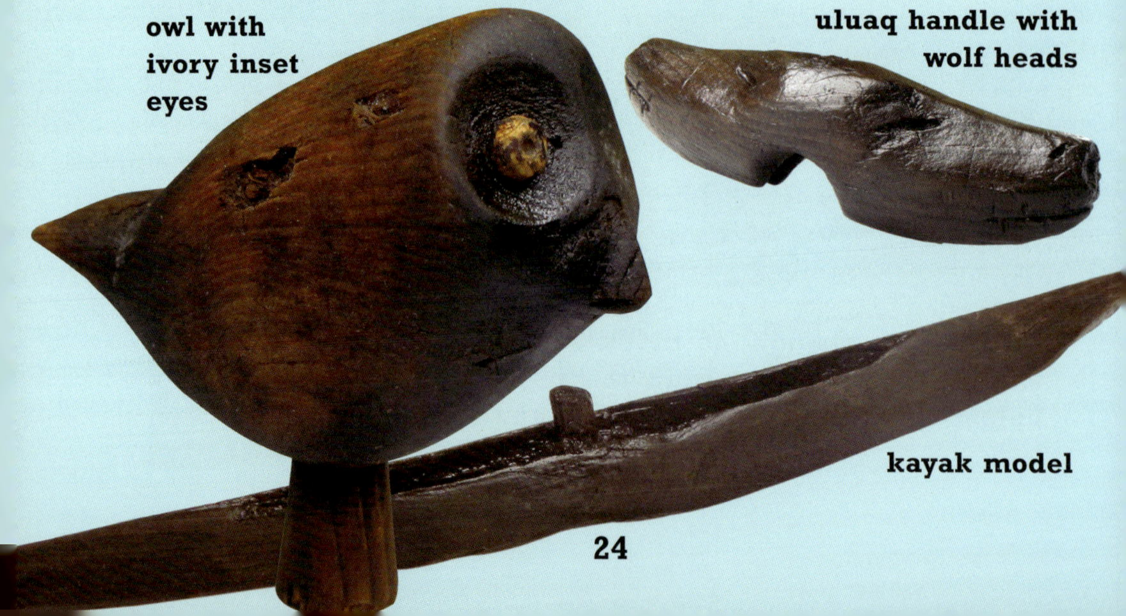

owl with ivory inset eyes

uluaq handle with wolf heads

kayak model

Knecht explained that the discovery answered many questions about the Yup'ik culture. "There are very few archaeological projects in this area, which is about the size of Great Britain. It's the biggest black hole in our knowledge of prehistory. There's been so little archaeology in Yup'ik country that everything we find here is a revelation."[7]

Archaeologist Charlotta Hillerdal is seen here with a mask that was found in Quinhagak in 2008. She and the rest of the team from the University of Aberdeen recovered more than 8,000 of these artifacts between 2009 and 2013.

CHAPTER FOUR

The Inupiaq and the St. Lawrence Island Yup'ik

The Alaska Native Heritage Center divides the Native Alaskan tribes from the northern and northwestern areas of the state between the Inupiaq and the St. Lawrence Island Yup'ik People. When they were first discovered by the Europeans, they consisted of five different smaller groups within the larger two. Their population at that time was nearly 10,000 individuals, with more than a third of them being the Inupiat in Kotzebue Sound.

The traditional cultures and customs of this region centered on families. But the various clans also interacted with one another regularly. Bartering, or trading one item or service for another, was especially common in this region. If a neighboring tribe needed something, it was wise for a nearby clan to help out whenever possible, for every tribe ended up in the position of needing something eventually.

Hunting and gathering is still a way of life here. The land is vast, with many mammals, birds, and fish. Surviving in this cold

The Alaskan climate demands tools made especially for its harsh environment. This Inupiaq hunts with a harpoon and travels through the icy waters in an umiaq (OO-mee-ak), a boat covered in seal skin.

Oftentimes the Yup'ik cannot use all the fish that the men catch before it spoils. To avoid wasting any of this vital resource, they dry a portion of it—like this salmon from the Kuskokwim River.

climate is not for the weak. It takes knowledge of the area and a great deal of strength and fortitude.

Native Alaskan Joan Naviyuk Kane is an award-winning poet and novelist who writes about the struggles of the northern Alaskan Natives. Through her work she helps her own Inupiaq culture carry on.

"Part of the reason why King Islanders were renowned carvers, singers, and dancers was because they had this supreme location for marine mammal hunting, so that part of survival was not a big issue," she explains. "My boys know a couple of dances. My 22-year-old niece, who is living with us now, is a fabulous, graceful Eskimo dancer. The only video she lets my boys put on is Eskimo dancing. I'm extremely ungainly and awkward," Kane laughs, "but I'm trying to learn."[1]

Her own work deals with a more serious side of life as a Native Alaskan. "In history, federal Indian policies moved from extermination to assimilation to the self-determination we see today," Kane says. "In 1959, which is also the year that Alaska became a state, it was the height of the assimilation era. Also, it was increasingly difficult to keep teachers out on King Island, and they finally shut down the school."[2]

In order to survive, Native American cultural practices must be passed from one generation to the next. Here, an elder Yup'ik woman teaches younger Native Alaskans how to do bead work at Akiak High School.

Many Native tribes continue to live off the land and waters off Alaska's coast. Animals such as whales, fish, and seals play a large role in their daily lives.

Kane credits her parents for supporting her interest in hanging onto her Inupiaq culture. "My mother's generation, people who lived on the island before relocation, are fully bilingual. I've been very fortunate to attend public schools in Anchorage and have my parents supportive of my wanting to learn things. My mother worked very hard to make me feel proud of who I was."[3]

Kane knew that not all her family members had been so lucky. "My grandfather never spoke a word of English," she reveals. "Providing for his ten children was entirely dependent on hunting seals and walrus and trading with mainlanders for reindeer and salmon. It was a very hard life. I don't know how to, say, split a walrus skin to make a kayak. I don't know how to do any of the things that were just a part of daily life."[4]

Another part of Kane's culture that she fears for is the King Island dialect of the Inupiaq language. Kane says she doesn't want to create an image of her Native people vanishing, "but the fact of the matter is that most of the people in my generation do not understand the dialect at all. My mother was emphatic about speaking the dialect to me."[5]

Out of all the different groups of Native Alaskan clans, the Yup'ik languages are still spoken by the most people. Linguist Michael Krauss is the founder of the Alaska Native Language Center. He has made it his life's work to document and preserve Alaska's twenty Native languages. As he explains, "Only Central Yup'ik is still spoken by children, in about a dozen villages out of about sixty. It's by no means a safe language, but it's the best in Alaska by far. There may be a minority of children on St. Lawrence Island, in Gambell and Savoonga, speaking Siberian Yup'ik." He adds, "When a language is no longer spoken by children, it will become extinct in a lifetime."[6]

So how has Central Yup'ik survived? "It was luckier than most," Krauss shares, "in that the area had almost no resources or harbors that white men were interested in. And it had a relatively large population to begin with that has gotten much larger. And it happened to attract Russian Orthodox, Roman Catholic, and Moravian missionaries who were quite interested and empathetic toward the language. For a while, missionaries reinforced the Central Yup'ik language, until American schools moved in and punished children for speaking their own language."[7]

Some people think that all Americans should speak a single language. But, as Krauss points out, "Languages are not merely different words for the same things. Each language is full of specialized information about the world that only those people have learned. And each language has its own take on the nature of our common existence. No human language is better than another in that regard."[8]

The problem is not unique to the Native Alaskans. "We're losing languages, worldwide, about one a week," shares Krauss. "It's unprecedented, mass extinction."[9]

Gambell is one of two villages on the island of St. Lawrence. Along with Savoonga, it is located on the island's north shore. But the villages do not interact with each other—or other parts of Alaska—much at all. The terrain between the villages contains no road. And the nearest town, Nome, is 150 miles away on the mainland.

Repeat After Me . . .

One of the reasons that Native Alaskan languages are difficult for some people to learn is that some letters are used in a variety of ways. The Inupiaq language, for example, includes only three vowels in its alphabet. But they can be used and pronounced a total of twelve different ways.

a = uh
aa= aahhh
ai= long a
au = oh

i= short i
ia= ee-uh
ii= eeeeeeeeeeee
iu= eee-oo

u= oo
ua = oo-uh
ui= oo-ee
uu= oooooooo

is a little thing that
Neat!

CHAPTER FIVE

The Eyak, Tlingit, Haida, and Tsimshian

The Alaska Native Heritage Center groups the Eyak, Tlingit, Haida, and Tsimshian peoples together mostly due to geography. The Eyak lived in the southeastern area of the state, along the Gulf of Alaska. But they actually came from farther inland. For this reason they have much in common with the Athabascans. The Tlingit tribe spanned southeastern coastal Alaska in the panhandle from Yakutat south to Ketchikan. Scientists have found this clan has lived in the area for about 10,000 years. The Haida people came from British Columbia, Canada, to just north of Prince of Wales Island. And the Tsimshian also came from British Columbia. Some parts of this clan remained in Canada, while others moved to Alaska's Annette Island.

Although these tribes were all located in the southeastern region of Alaska, they didn't have much interaction with one another. Surely, traditional life as members of these clans meant hunting the same animals and gathering the same types of plants. But their daily lives were completely separate. The tribes didn't even understand one another's languages.

Sadly, the Eyak language is thought to have died in 2008 when the last known full-blooded Eyak tribe member—and the language's only speaker—passed away. Shortly after Marie Smith Jones' death, journalist Mark Abley wrote, "Jones married a white man, and did not pass on her language to her children—a decision she came to regret. But she made it to spare them the pain she had endured. As a girl, she had learned to see bilingualism not as an asset but an impediment. Eyak, she had been told, was a useless language."[1]

One of the few things these clans did have in common was their lack of government. Whenever a problem arose within one of the tribes, it was handled within the village where the issue took place or within an individual home. Despite having no tribal governments, the southeastern clans divided their members into classes. A few families ranked at the top of this system. Most of the people, though, were what we might think of as commoners. Both classes kept slaves—people they had kidnapped during raids on nearby villages.

Today members of these tribes decide whom, when, and if they want to marry. But traditionally, marriages were arranged by families. When a marriage took place, the husband would join his new wife's family and the children automatically became part of that group. This practice was very different from the European way, in which children inherited their names (and often their property rights) from their fathers. In these Native Alaskan clans, the mothers' identities determined the children's future. The class a person belonged to, where one could fish and hunt, and even one's clothing was determined by the mother's side of the family.

Although many parts of life for the southeastern tribes changed over time, many things remain the same to this day. Many families put food on the table by hunting caribou, moose, and seal. Beaver trapping is also common. Berry picking and egg hunting may sound like something that tribes did many years ago, but these activities are also still an important part of life in southern Alaska. Particularly in the winter when shopping at a store means driving on ice, finding one's own food is a much more practical choice. Even children, many of whom receive their first gun around the age of eight, take part in hunting.

Growing up in this remote environment is very different from living in other parts of the United States. Although Native Alaskans are Native Americans, their experiences differ greatly from members of other Native American tribes. Tlingit tribe member Grace Denning is currently attending Haskell Indian Nations University

Scenic Glacier Bay is located on the Alaskan panhandle.

in Lawrence, Kansas. She and fellow student Daniel Andrew are two of only about a dozen Native Alaskans in the entire school. Living away from home is often a big adjustment for most college students, but in Denning's and Andrew's case, the changes have been extreme.

Denning is from the islands near Juneau. Back home even simple trips involved both time and planning. "You have to take a plane or a ferry or some type of boat. . . . I'm not used to being able to drive to Wal-Mart," she said.[2]

Both students have had a hard time adjusting to the climate of their new, temporary home. Denning describes Lawrence as "almost unbearably hot and humid."[3]

Although the Alaskan climate intimidates many people, it draws certain adventurous people into the area. Southeastern Alaska is a popular tourist destination. In 2011, about 876,000 people boarded cruise ships that took them to Juneau—a city with a population of only 31,000.[4]

The breathtaking views of the mountains and glaciers are among the reasons many tourists choose to visit southeastern Alaska. Visitors who want to do their own fishing can charter small boats

For much of the United States, fall is deer hunting season. In Alaska, however, one of the most popular animals to hunt is the caribou.

or book weeklong expeditions on yachts that specialize in the activity.

Even people who have no interest in fishing may enjoy taking a boat or ferry ride. Dave Berg owns Viking Travel in Petersburg. He points out, "Whale watching is really good out of here." Berg can even help tourists find businesses that offer bear viewing trips. "You can walk the docks and see the different types of fishing boats. You can enjoy local seafood at the restaurants."[5]

David Moorehead is the chef at the Gold Room at the Westmark Baranog hotel. In addition to clams, halibut, and scallops, he prepares three different types of crab and two types of salmon. One of them is white salmon, which is extremely rare. Moorehead explains, "[It] is only found in southeast Alaska. It's a very unique fish with a very interesting flavor . . . a fresh ocean flavor."[6]

Many Alaskans living in smaller villages want to make sure they don't grow too much from tourism. Part of the charm, after all, is the size of the communities. Sally Dwyer is director of the Petersburg Chamber of Commerce. She notes, "We get about fifty people a week that come to our visitor center and say, 'We were on the ferry and decided to stop here.'"[7]

Many tourists who embark on a whale watching tour in Alaska are lucky enough to see orcas.

The Code Talkers

The Tlingit tribe played an important role in the victory of World War II. During the war, the United States faced a serious challenge in creating codes the country's enemies could not break. Each time a code was created, the Japanese quickly cracked it. This weakness made it impossible for commanders to communicate with soldiers without the Japanese knowing what the next move would be.

In 1942, though, the US discovered an invaluable resource that until then had been overlooked. Many Native American languages had never been recorded in writing. Unknown to the Japanese, words from these languages could be used without any risk of the enemy figuring out the new code. Twenty-nine Native Americans from numerous tribes helped create a new code that was never broken. The "code talkers," as they are called, are credited with saving thousands of lives and helping the US and its allies win the war.

In 2013, Congress held a ceremony to honor the Native Americans who took part in this significant project. William "Ozzie" Sheakley accepted a medal for his late uncle, Richard Bean Sr., who was one of five code talkers from the Tlingit tribe. In all the years following the war, Bean never discussed his role in the project with anyone. "He took his job very seriously," his nephew noted.[8]

In 2013, the United States government awarded the Native American "code talkers" with the Congressional Gold Medal for their service. Surviving family members accepted the honor on their late relatives' behalf.

Chapter Six
Does Oil Drilling Threaten Native Alaskan Cultures?

Long before Alaska became the 49th US state in 1959, the area was known as America's last frontier. With so much undeveloped territory, Alaska is seen by many Americans as a potentially vital resource for the future. With the rising cost of fossil fuels imported from the Middle East, Americans are facing an economic crisis when it comes to filling their cars' gas tanks and heating their homes. But the problem is also an environmental one.

Oil companies want to drill in Alaska. In fact some already have. These businesses think that a great deal of oil exists deep within the ground there. The subject of drilling has become an issue of enormous debate. People who are concerned about the environment insist that more drilling would hurt both people and wildlife. Many Alaskans depend on the land for their livelihoods, and many animals in the region are also already threatened or endangered. Some people think that drilling would only worsen this problem. Others think it is possible to find and collect oil without harming either the humans or the animals. Native Alaskans, whose families have lived in the region, are equally divided on the subject.

Alaskan Native Rosemary Ahtuangaruak is an Inupiaq—and an activist for the environment. She sees the primary motivation behind drilling as money. "Others have goals of lofty wants out there," she notes. "But when it's the goals of protecting who and what we are as a people, and keeping us healthy in our tradition and cultures, this is a conflict that we cannot meet."[1]

Ahtuangaruak worries about how she would put food on the table if the oil companies get their way. Many families in the region rely heavily on hunting and fishing. "We need the foods from our lands and waters to feed our families" she explains. "We cannot afford to buy the foods that come up to the Arctic. The costs of transportation increase these costs, so that it can take your whole paycheck to try to feed your family from the store."[2]

Former Point Hope mayor Caroline Cannon points out that whaling is an important part of Native Alaskan culture. "We rely on the whale, the bowhead whale. It is our identity. It is who we are, and the thought of offshore drilling, or an oil spill, is very terrifying."[3]

This bowhead mother and calf are just one of the marine species that could suffer as a result of drilling for oil in Arctic waters.

Edward Itta is a former mayor of North Slope Borough, Alaska. When he campaigned for the office, he too opposed drilling. "My initial attitude was . . . [O]ver my dead body," he said. But as he began serving as mayor, he realized that the issue was more complicated than he had thought. The local governments need money to pay for everything the area needs. And the number of things on that list has increased a lot over the last several decades. "Our tax base is based on oil and gas. There's nothing else there," he reports. "We have schools, airports, roads, landfills, health facilities, hospitals, decent homes which keep warm now and have light and power, which when I grew up we didn't have."[4]

Itta sees drilling as a necessity. But he doesn't deny that it could come with a great cost. He says he definitely worries about a spill. But he is more concerned that Alaska could miss an important financial opportunity by not getting involved in drilling. "If there was no economic benefit up there, we would be opposed, period."[5]

The debate reaches much further than the state of Alaska. In fact it has gone all the way to the US 9th Circuit Court of Appeals. In January of 2014, the federal court ruled in favor of a group that is suing the US Department of the Interior over the situation. Made up of several environmental groups and Native Alaskans against drilling, the group claimed that the government illegally opened nearly thirty million acres to the Shell Oil Company. But the court's decision was not unanimous, and Shell will likely appeal it. It could take months or even years for a final decision on the matter.

Oliver Leavitt is a former vice president of the Arctic Slope Regional Corporation, a regional Native corporation created by Congress under the Alaska Native Claims Settlement Act of 1971. He is also the leader of a whaling clan in Barrow. Leavitt insists that Barrow owes much of its development to previous drilling in Alaska. He states, "The infrastructure that you see in Barrow is what was brought in by oil. Before the discovery of oil, there was no education past eighth grade. This place has been transformed because of oil."[6]

Leavitt also thinks that the younger generations of Native people in Barrow have moved past hunting and fishing. In fact, he doubts that many young people even know how to live off the land the way their ancestors did. "A lot of the young say they will go back to the old ways." But he counters, "They don't know the old way. They grew up with the oil money."[7]

Whether they are passing their customs down to their children or not, many Native people are still relying on the Alaskan waters for their food. One of them is Ron Saganna, a member of the Patkotak whaling crew. "That's our garden out there," he says of the Beaufort Sea, a small section of the Arctic Ocean. "Over 50 percent of our food source comes from the ocean."[8]

Some scientists assert that drilling in Alaska isn't just bad for the Native Alaskans, but also a waste of time. Jeff Short is the Pacific science director for Oceana, an ocean conservation

Oil revenue has helped the state of Alaska pay for many of its modern resources, such as schools like this high school in the city of Barrow.

Oil drilling has already changed the look of the seascape in Alaska. This artificial landmass called Northstar Island was established for the purpose of oil and gas drilling. It is located in the Beaufort Sea.

organization based in Washington D.C. He explains, "The U.S. Minerals Management Service (MMS) estimates there are twenty-two billion barrels of recoverable reserves in the Beaufort and Chukchi seas. If even a portion were exploited, it would be far more than what is currently produced in the state of Alaska. If the total twenty-two billion barrels were somehow recovered and produced—which is an almost negligible likelihood—it would be enough oil to supply all the U.S.'s [current level of consumption] for three years. It's really more like six months once you get down to what they're likely to recover, though. As far as world consumption is concerned, that goes down to a week or so. So drilling off of

Alaska is not something that's going to save us as far as energy security and supply goes. It's just one more quick fix."[9]

Additionally, Short joins many other scientists in worrying about the effects that drilling could have on global warming. Drilling would reduce the surface area of the sea ice, which helps maintain global temperatures. Water absorbs more sunlight and heat than ice does. And the effects of this warmer water then spread to landmasses. Eventually, large amounts of methane and carbon dioxide would be released, causing additional melting.

"These are the kind of things that keep me up at night," Short shares. "I have a twelve-year-old kid and I despair thinking of what kind of planet he will be dealing with when he's my age. It is just crazy to me why we are considering doing this in Alaska when we may set in motion events that we will never be able to stop."[10]

Many Native Alaskans worry about what increased drilling would do to their natural environment. They want to keep the beauty and resources, such as those of the Arctic National Wildlife Refuge, unspoiled for future generations.

The *Exxon Valdex* Disaster

Worries over oil spills aren't just a matter of people imagining the worst. For many Alaskans, the devastating effects of an oil spill are engraved in their memories. On March 24, 1989, the *Exxon Valdez* oil tanker accidentally dumped 40,000 tons of oil into the waters of Prince William Sound, Alaska. The toxic substance spread over 10,000 square miles of ocean water, reaching 1,300 miles of Alaska's coastline. Among the areas affected were national parks, wildlife refuges, national forestland, and the ancestral lands of Native Alaskans.

The *Huffington Post*'s Richard Steiner writes, "The risks of offshore drilling are real. For the Arctic, the administration last year released its own modeling for a 'very large oil spill' from an exploration wellhead blowout that would continue for seventy-four days, spill over two million barrels of oil, spread over 200,000 square miles (an area larger than the state of California), and oil over 850 miles of shoreline, even spreading into Russian waters. They assure us that this is only a remote possibility,

there is a good oil spill response plan, and that 95 percent of any oil spill would be recovered."[11] Should we believe these promises?

Walter Meganack is the traditional Village Chief of the Port Graham Native Village. Shortly after the *Exxon Valdez* spill, he wrote, "The oil companies lied about preventing the spill. Now they lie about the clean-up. Our people know what happens on the beaches. Spend all day cleaning one huge rock and the tide comes in and it's covered with oil again. Spend a week wiping and spraying the surface, but pick up a rock and there's four inches of oil underneath."[12]

Despite the bleakness of the situation, Meganack remained hopeful for the future. "I am an elder. I am chief. I will not lose hope. I will help my people. We have never lived through this kind of death, but we have lived through lots of other kinds of death. We will learn from the past, we will learn from each other, and we will live. The water is dead, but we are alive, and where there is life there is hope."[13]

Chapter Seven
Climate and Culture

The topic of global warming is one that many people—even scientists—debate regularly. The arguments range from who is to blame for the rising temperatures within the earth's atmosphere to whether global warming even exists at all. In 2011, presidential candidate Rick Santorum declared, "There is no such thing as global warming."[1]

In 2013, *Forbes* magazine's James Taylor wrote about a survey conducted by the journal *Organizational Studies*. Taylor reported that "a strong majority of the 1,077 respondents believe that nature is the primary cause of recent global warming and/or that future global warming will not be a very serious problem."[2]

But that same year, a survey conducted by the journal *Environmental Research Letters* was made public. More than 4,000 papers taking a position on global warming were reviewed for the project. And more than 97 percent of them asserted that human beings are responsible for global warming.[3] It can be difficult to know what the truth is.

It can also be tough to understand how global warming is happening when we experience an especially brutal winter. Marshall Shepherd is the former head of the American Meteorological Society. He shares, "When we get winter weather, cold conditions, you know, you've got some that will say, 'Well, what are you guys worried about climate change or global warming? I mean, it's cold and snowing.' And I'll say, 'You know, it's winter. It's January or February. We get snowstorms.'"[4]

Shepherd explains that it is important to consider the seasons. "That's like saying, because it's night time, the sun doesn't exist anymore. On the other hand, though, there is evidence—there's some scientific literature that suggests that jet stream patterns can be affected by the amplified warming that we're seeing up in the Arctic because of climate change or global warming. Now, that's real. We know that climate change is happening and humans are contributing. I'm not quite ready to say that this snowstorm we saw this week or last week is caused by global warming or climate change, but one thing I will emphasize, I think we've forgotten how to be cold or deal with snowstorms because we're seeing so few of these big storms like we've seen, and that probably is because of climate warming."[5]

If you live in a warmer part of the United States, you may not notice much of a difference in temperatures each year. Many people may even wonder why increasing warmth is a problem. But in Alaska, the issue of global warming is much easier to notice.

Ignatius Rigor is a climatologist at the University of Washington's Polar Ice Center. "This is the front line of global climate change," he states. "You know, basically before the planet can heat up, you have to—just like your glass of water, before it can get warm, you have to get rid of the ice. And so we are seeing the ice disappear and we are seeing the Arctic Ocean start to warm up. . . . This ice is melting away dramatically. Each summer, we have lost more than half of the ice cover that we typically have. And we have lost a lot of the thickness of sea ice. And so, taken together, the total volume of sea ice is down to less than 40 percent of what it used to be."[6]

Why is the melting ice a problem? PBS News Hour producer April Brown explains, "For centuries, what's known as multi-year ice, or the accumulation of sea ice from one year to the next, has been crucial to life [in Alaska]. It provides whaling captains like Harry Brower the peace of mind to know that his crew can stand on thick ice while hunting whales, something Inupiats still have special permission to do. But in the past few years, Brower says he's seen mostly stretches of small, shallow ice that are extremely dangerous for hunters, and because of the conditions, the community has struggled to reach its annual quota."[7]

Whalers pull a bowhead whale onto ice using a block and tackle pulley system in the Chukchi Sea off the shores of Barrow, Alaska.

Brower said, "Last spring was very poor. We didn't even harvest one [whale] for Barrow throughout the whole migratory season."[8]

Many Alaskans fear that if something isn't done soon, the problem could reach a point of no return. Mike Donovan, a resident of Barrow, Alaska, said, "[I]t's kind of hard to say if our younger generations will be able to do what we do."[9]

Brown points out that some opportunities can be found amidst the rising temperatures. "Even though the melting sea ice is changing the way a lot of residents here on the North Slope of Alaska go about their traditions, it's also bringing economic

Many scientists insist that glaciers are at risk of disappearing from the waters off Alaska due to global warming.

opportunities. Sea routes once blocked by layers of impenetrable ice have recently begun opening, and many corporations are eying ways to push further into the resource-rich Arctic. Oil and gas companies already operating in the region pay taxes that finance the North Slope boroughs' $350 million annual budget."[10] But will those opportunities be enough to save Alaska's economy? And how will all this change affect Native Alaskan cultures?

Rigor admits, "The local populations are torn because they realize that there is a bounty off their coast that could really improve their lifestyle, but those bounties also could be catastrophic for their way of life. And if an accident happens, you know, there goes subsistence hunting and whaling."[11]

Some residents, like Donovan, can't be swayed. "Even if they paid me a million dollars or $100 million," he vows, "I wouldn't trade this lifestyle for anything in the world."[12]

So Goes Alaska, So Goes the World

Former North Slope mayor Edward Itta states, "Barrow is ground zero for climate-change science. We worry that climate change is shrinking the sea ice and we don't know how that will affect the animals that depend on it."[13]

Long-term effects cannot be fully understood until they actually happen. But people who work with wildlife offer insight into how warming might affect the animals. For example, University of Washington oceanographer Kate Stafford explains, "Marine mammals use sound to communicate and navigate. When the water is covered with ice it's pretty quiet down there. During spring breakup it gets noisy. If the ice becomes thinner in winters or goes away, it may become more difficult for animals to communicate."[14]

The problem of global warming affects us all—from Native Alaskans to the animals who inhabit the region to people who live hundreds and even thousands of miles away. Dan Endres ran the National Oceanic and Atmospheric Administration in Barrow for twenty-five years. He warns, "[A] small change in the temperature in the Arctic can produce greater changes than in lower latitudes. Whatever is going to happen in the rest of the world happens first and to the greatest extent in the Arctic. The Arctic is the mirror of the world."[15]

The United Nations Climate Change Conference, 2013

Experiencing Native Alaskan Culture

To experience Native Alaskan cultures firsthand, one must either travel to the state of Alaska or have a personal connection to one of the many Native Alaskan tribes. Tribe members who leave Alaska often move to the lower United States to go to college or begin a new job. Once there, the culture in their new homes often replaces the ways these Native Alaskans grew up doing things. They do not lose their family history, of course, but their old ways usually do not become part of their new environment. Many Native Alaskans worry that their cultural identity will be lost when they leave their northern homes.

Traveling to the more remote areas of Alaska isn't for everyone. The weather can be harsh and even transportation can require a great deal of planning involving several different stages. A visitor's best bet for experiencing Native Alaskan culture is spending time in one of that state's biggest communities. These areas, such as Anchorage, Fairbanks, and Juneau, might not seem like cities at all to Americans used to a more bustling metropolis like New York or Chicago. But they offer a blending of modern convenience and traditional customs—all while being more accessible than the more remote regions.

A visit to the Alaska Native Heritage Center in Anchorage provides an opportunity to learn about all eleven of the state's Native Alaskan cultures. The educational and cultural institution covers twenty-six acres of land located on the edge of a scenic lake. Guests can tour Native housing, take part in interactive displays, and watch films about Native peoples and their traditions while there.

Map of Alaska

TIMELINE

1778	Captain James Cook explores the Arctic Ocean
1784	The first white settlers arrive in Alaska on Kodiak Island.
1799	Czar Paul claims Alaska as a Russian possession.
	Aleksandr Baranov becomes the first Russian governor of Alaska.
1835	England and the United States begin trading with Alaska.
1843	The Russian-Greek Orthodox Church opens the first mission school for Native Alaskans at Nushagak.
1848	Americans begin whaling in Alaskan waters.
1867	Alaska becomes part of the United States.
1880	Gold is discovered near Juneau.
1896	Gold is discovered in Canada's Yukon Territory, bringing prospectors by boat to Alaska on their way to the Yukon for what became known as the Klondike Gold Rush.
1902	Gold is discovered near Fairbanks.
1924	The Indian Citizenship Act grants citizenship to all Native Americans.
1942	The relocation of many Native Alaskans takes place.
1942–1945	The Native American "code talkers" save American lives and help the US win World War II.
1946	The Alaskan people vote to apply for statehood.
1959	Alaska becomes the 49th US state.
1973	The Iditarod Trail Sled Dog Race takes place for the first time.
1989	The *Exxon Valdez* oil tanker spills 40,000 tons of oil into Prince William Sound, Alaska.
2013	Congress holds a ceremony to honor the Native American "code talkers," although many of them were no longer living.
2014	A federal court ruling keeps the Shell Oil Company from drilling in Alaska—at least for the time being. Appeals in the case between environmental groups and the US Department of the Interior continue.

CHAPTER NOTES

Chapter 1. The Athabascans

1. O'Malley, Julia. "Share, stock, hoard: What do you do with your fish?" *Anchorage Daily News*, June 17, 2011 – http://www.adn.com/2011/06/17/1922825/the-etiquitte-of-fishing-is-it.html.
2. Ibid.
3. Ibid.
4. Johnson, Kirk. "Tribe Revives Language On Verge of Extinction." *New York Times*, August 4, 2012.
5. Ibid.
6. Ibid.
7. Anonymous. "Alaskan Dallas Seavey wins 2014 Iditarod Sled Dog Race in record time." Associated Press, March 11, 2014 – http://www.theguardian.com/world/2014/mar/11/iditarod-sled-dog-race-alaska-dallas-seavey.

Chapter 2: The Unangax and Alutiiq

1. Dixon, Martha. "Religious legacy lives on in Alaska." BBC, Alaska, September 12, 2004 – http://news.bbc.co.uk/2/hi/americas/3531458.stm.
2. Ibid.
3. Anonymous. "Evacuation and Internment, 1942-1945." National Park Service – http://www.nps.gov/aleu/historyculture/unangan-internment.htm.
4. Ibid.
5. Braun, David. "For Alaska's Alutiiq, the Future May Be Found in the Past." *National Geographic*, August 1, 2011 – http://newswatch.nationalgeographic.com/2011/08/01/for-alaskas-alutiiq-the-future-may-be-found-in-the-past/.
6. Ibid.
7. Ibid.

Chapter 3: The Yup'ik and Cup'ik

1. D'Oro, Rachel. "With ban lifted, Eskimo dancing embraced in Alaskan village." *The Charleston Gazette*, February 22, 2010.
2. Ibid.
3. Ibid.
4. Dunham, Mike. "Unearthing relics of Alaska's past: Excavation reveals largest treasure trove of Yup'ik artifacts." *South Florida Sun Sentinel*, August 28, 2013.
5. Ibid.
6. Ibid.
7. Ibid.

Chapter 4: The Inupiaq and the St. Lawrence Island Yup'ik

1. Weideman, Paul. "Lines from the north: Poet and novelist Joan Naviyuk Kane." *Tribune Business News*, February 7, 2014.
2. Ibid.
3. Ibid.
4. Ibid.
5. Ibid.
6. Ibid.
7. Cox, Rose. "Linguist raises voice for preservation of Native tongues." *Anchorage Daily News*, November 14, 2007.
8. Ibid.
9. Ibid.
10. Ibid.

Chapter 5: The Eyak, Tlingit, Haida, and Tsimshian

1. Abley, Mark. "G2: 'It's like bombing the Louvre': Marie Smith Jones was the world's last Eyak speaker - by the time she died last week, she could use her mother tongue only in her dreams. But the loss of a language is not just a personal tragedy, says Mark Abley, it is a cultural disaster." *The Guardian*, January 28, 2008.
2. Shepherd, Sara. Alaska natives find Kan. to be different." *The Hutchinson News*, Janaury 11, 2014.
3. Ibid.
4. Jones, Jay. "Alaska cruise lite: For adventurous souls, modest ferries offer unique access at a bargain rate away from crowds." *Chicago Tribune*, February 19, 2012.
5. Ibid.
6. Ibid.
7. Ibid.

CHAPTER NOTES

8. Hotakainen, Rob. "Congress Honors 33 Native American Tribes for Creating Secret War Codes." *Pittsburgh Post-Gazette*, November 24, 2013.

Chapter 6: Does Oil Drilling Threaten Native Alaskan Cultures?

1. Harris, Richard. "Native Alaskans Divided On State's Oil Drilling Debate." National Public Radio, March 12, 2012 – http://www.npr.org/2012/03/20/148754357/native-alaskans-divided-on-states-oil-drilling-debate.
2. Ibid.
3. Ibid.
4. Ibid.
5. Ibid.
6. Dlouhy, Jennifer A. "Can Arctic culture survive oil?" *The Courier* (Houma, Louisiana), November 23, 2012.
7. Ibid.
8. Ibid.
9. Hadhazy, Adam. "Drilling the Arctic for Energy: Does tapping Alaskan oil to increase energy independence come at our peril?" *Scientific American*, March 24, 2009 – http://www.scientificamerican.com/article/drilling-the-arctic-for-energy/.
10. Ibid.
11. Steiner, Richard. "Exxon Valdez Oil Spill a Cautionary Tale for Arctic Ocean Drilling." *Huffington Post*, March 24, 2012 – http://www.huffingtonpost.com/richard-steiner/exxon-valdez-oil-spill_b_1377011.html.
12. National Wildlife Federation, Chief Walter Meganack on Native Alaskan Life in the Wake of the Exxon Valdez Oil Spill – https://www.nwf.org/What-We-Do/Protect-Habitat/Gulf-Restoration/Oil-Spill/Effects-on-Wildlife/Compare-Exxon-Valdez-and-BP-Oil-Spills/Day-the-Water-Died-Essay.aspx.
13. Ibid.

Chapter 7: Climate and Culture

1. Costello, Carol. "Why are we still debating climate change?" CNN, February 24, 2014.
2. Taylor, James. "Peer-Reviewed Survey Finds Majority Of Scientists Skeptical Of Global Warming Crisis." *Forbes*, February 13, 2013 – http://www.forbes.com/sites/jamestaylor/2013/02/13/peer-reviewed-survey-finds-majority-of-scientists-skeptical-of-global-warming-crisis/.
3. Nuccitelli, Dana. "Survey finds 97% of climate science papers agree warming is man-made." *The Guardian*, May 16, 2013 – http://www.theguardian.com/environment/climate-consensus-97-per-cent/2013/may/16/climate-change-scienceofclimatechange.
4. Bob Schieffer Hosts CBS Face the Nation (transcript), February 16, 2014.
5. Ibid.
6. PBS NewsHour (transcript), September 18, 2013.
7. Ibid.
8. Ibid.
9. Ibid.
10. Ibid.
11. Ibid.
12. Ibid.
13. Reiss, Bob. "Barrow, Alaska: Ground Zero for Climate Change." Smithsonian.com, March 2010 – http://www.smithsonianmag.com/science-nature/barrow-alaska-ground-zero-for-climate-change-7553696/?page=1.
14. Ibid.
15. Ibid.

FURTHER READING

Books

Corral, Roy. *What the Elders Have Taught Us: Alaska Native Ways.* Portland, Oregon: Alaska Northwest Books, 2013.

Funk, Joe. *Mush! The Sled Dogs of the Iditarod.* New York, New York: Scholastic, 2013.

Santella, Andrew. *Navajo Code Talkers.* Madison, Wisconsin: We The People, 2004.

On the Internet

Alaska Native Heritage Center, http://www.alaskanative.net/

Alaskool Central, http://www.alaskool.org/

University of Fairbanks, Native Alaskan Cultures http://fna.community.uaf.edu/alaska-native-cultures/

Works Consulted

Alaska Native Heritage Center, http://www.alaskanative.net/en/main-nav/education-and-programs/cultures-of-alaska/

Anonymous. "Urban Unangax Culture Camp." Aleutian Pribiliof Tribal Association, http://www.apiai.org/culture-history/culture-camp/

Anonymous. "Historic Iditarod." *Scholastic News*, http://teacher.scholastic.com/activities/iditarod/historic/index.asp?article=historic_iditarod

Anonymous. "The Forum: The Iditarod is a stone cold challenge." *The Nationalist*, April 4, 2013.

The Library of Congress, Treaty with Russia for the Purchase of Alaska, http://www.loc.gov/rr/program/bib/ourdocs/Alaska.html

Macalister, Terry. "Shell's Arctic drilling set back by US court ruling." *The Guardian*, January 23, 2014, http://www.theguardian.com/business/2014/jan/23/shell-arctic-drilling-set-back-us-court

Oyate Ta Olowan, The Atka Dancers/Unungax from Atka, Alaska, http://www.oyate.com/the-atka-dancers—unungax.html

The View From the North (blog), http://steveandangiealston.blogspot.com/2009/05/fun-fact-inupiaq-alphabet.html

Photo Credits: All design elements from Thinkstock/Sharon Beck; Cover—pp. 1, 6, 30, 38, 39, 42, 43, 54, 57—Thinkstock; p. 3—Thomas Sbampato imageBROKER/Newscom; pp. 7, 28, 29—Design Pics/Kevin Smith/Newscom; pp. 8, 10, 36—cc by sa: Diane Cordell; pp. 9, 15, 20, 23, 45, 55—cc-by-sa; p. 13—Bob Hallinen/ZUMA Press/Newscom; p. 14—Library of Congress, HABS AK,9-NINI,1—14 (CT); p. 16—National Archives, 80-G-12163; p. 17—akg-images/Newscom; p. 18—AP Photo/David Minthorn; p. 19—Federal Highway Administration, Christopher Mertl; p. 21—John Greim/LightRocket via Getty Images; pp. 24, 25—Rick Knecht, courtesy of Qanirtuuq, Inc.; p. 26—AlaskaNative.net; p. 27—Luciana Whitaker/LatinContent/Getty Images; pp. 32–33—State of Alaska Division of Community & Regional Affairs; p. 34 (inset), 34–35—Design Pics/Jeff Schultz/Newscom; p. 40—Stuart Westmorland/DanitaDelimont.com "Danita Delimont Photography"/Newscom; p. 41—J.M. Eddins, Jr./MCT/Newscom; p. 46—Joint Pipeline Office; p. 47—U.S. Fish and Wildlife Service; p. 48 (inset), 48–49—Exxon Valdez Oil Spill Trustee Council; p. 50—Patrick Endres/Newscom; pp. 52–53—Steve Kazlowski/DanitaDelimont "Danita Delimont Photography"/Newscom; p. 56—Mark Stadsklev/Newscom.

GLOSSARY

abomination (uh-bom-uh-NEY-shuhn)—Something detestable.

anthropology (an-thruh-POL-uh-jee)—The science of human beings and especially of their physical characteristics, their origin, their environment and social relations, and their culture.

archipelago (arh-kuh-PEL-uh-goh)—A group of islands.

assimilation (uh-sim-uh-LEY-shuhn)—The process of taking in new information or experiences and incorporating them into our existing ideas.

bilingual (bahy-LING-gwuhl)—Able to use two languages especially with fluency.

economy (ih-KON-uh-mee)—The management of financial resources within a country, state, or other region.

exterminate (ik-STUR-muh-neyt)—To get rid of something completely.

hierarchy (HAHY-uh-rahr-kee)—An arrangement into a series according to rank.

infrastructure (IN-FRUH-struhk-cher)—The system of public works of a country, state, or other region.

linguistics (ling-GWIS-tiks)—The study of human speech including the units, nature, structure, and development of language, languages, or a language.

permafrost (PUR-muh-frawst)—A permanently frozen layer at variable depth below the surface in frigid regions of the earth.

philosophy (fi-LOS-uh-fee)—Someone's basic beliefs about the way people should live.

INDEX

About the Author

Tammy Gagne is the author of numerous books for both adults and children, including *Life on the Reservations* and *Preserving Their Heritage* for Mitchell Lane Publishers. One of her favorite pastimes is visiting schools to speak to children about the writing process. She resides in northern New England with her husband, son, and a menagerie of animals.